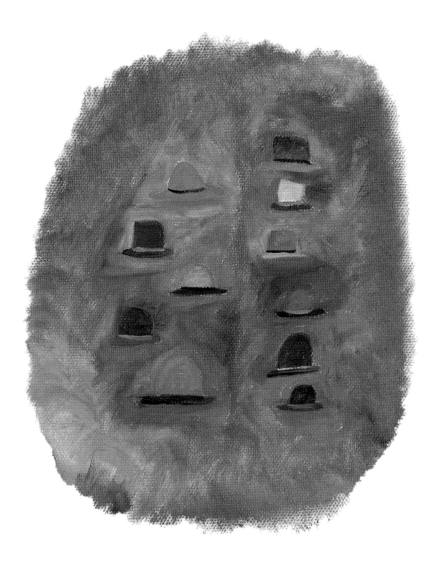

The Secret Legacy

·

Rigoberta Menchú

WITH Dante Liano

PICTURES BY

Domi

TRANSLATED BY David Unger

GROUNDWOOD BOOKS
HOUSE OF ANANSI PRESS
TORONTO   BERKELEY

Text copyright © 2006 by Rigoberta Menchú with Dante Liano
Illustrations copyright © 2008 by Domi
English translation copyright © 2008 by David Unger
Published in Canada and the USA in 2008 by Groundwood Books

Groundwood Books / House of Anansi Press
110 Spadina Avenue, Suite 801, Toronto, Ontario M5V 2K4
or c/o Publishers Group West
1700 Fourth Street, Berkeley, CA 94710

We acknowledge for their financial support of our publishing program the Government of Canada
through the Book Publishing Industry Development Program (BPIDP).

Library and Archives Canada Cataloguing in Publication
Menchú, Rigoberta
The Secret Legacy / Rigoberta Menchu with Dante Liano; pictures by Domi;
translated by David Unger.
Translation of: El legado secreto
ISBN-13: 978-0-88899-896-5
ISBN-10: 0-88899-896-1
1. Maya mythology–Juvenile literature. 2. Mayas–Folklore.
I. Liano, Dante II. Domi III. Unger, David IV. Title.
PZ8.1.M53Se 2008   j398.2089'974207281   C2008-902512-1

Design by Michael Solomon
The illustrations are in oils.
Printed and bound in China

Table of Contents

The Secret Legacy

The Hut in the Forest

THERE WAS once a little girl named Ixkem who lived with her grandfather in a thatched hut surrounded by flowers, plants and animals, deep in the forest. Tall trees grew all around, especially pine trees, whose tops swayed in the blue sky and dropped their needles, sharp as hummingbird tails, to the ground.

Before daybreak, the birds began to chatter so loudly that they'd awaken the biggest sleepyhead. Mockingbirds, robins, nightingales, canaries, woodpeckers and grackles chirped all together, while parrots squawked back and forth. The parakeets, who are downright useless for small talk, simply cheeped. They're so stupid that they often fall from the branches headfirst to the ground and *boing!* bounce upright as if they had springs. Then they start tottering around until they have the strength to fly back up and start the whole process over again.

Well, the forest birds weren't the only creatures waking up. Hens began to cluck and roosters went on with their cock-a-doodle-dooing, which they'd begun much earlier.

Why is it that roosters always crow before daybreak and keep it up long after the sun has risen?

And the dog barked at the butterfly that he'd been trying to snap with his muzzle. And the pigs made their oinkety, oinks! The rabbits, on the other hand, were as quiet as mice, secretly chewing lettuce leaves as if they were doing something wrong. Then the sun rose, and the world of birds went off to its business and amusement.

The shrubs awoke drenched by the night dew-keeper — a damp spirit that flies over plants, coating them with water. Its trail of droplets provided thousands of mirrors for the sun, which slipped between the trees like a cinnamon stick and sparked splinters of light.

A spiral of smoke from the firewood used to make breakfast rose from the hut and danced softly in the air, tickled by the wind. Since the grandfather was now very old, the little girl cooked breakfast. The crackling fire, the grindstone, the pan and the coffee were on the floor near the beds where they slept. She made beans with chile, a few tortillas and a large pot of coffee that smelled of morning and newly dug-up clay.

The grandfather was so happy to sit and slowly eat his tortillas and beans — each bite accompanied by a sip of hot coffee. It was as if the world were saying to him: "I'm here to give you my harvest. Warm your stomach and strengthen your soul. The forest and fields are here for your pleasure. They've been born again so you can ask permission to walk among them and receive the gifts of this marvelous creation!"

And what a great pleasure it was for Ixkem to serve her old grandfather and eat with him!

The world was opening to her as her grandfather took her by the hand into the countryside to learn the secrets of the earth. This was the grandfather's plan — to pass the secret legacy of his wisdom along to the girl. And that's why the girl existed — to receive this secret legacy from her grandfather.

A path from the hut led a little way deeper, but not too far, into the forest and then ended at a field where the grandfather grew corn.

The ritual for planting the corn did not begin today or yesterday or the day before yesterday or even last week. The planting ritual began long before the grandfather was born. It began long before his own grandmother and grandfather had appeared and before his great-grandfather had had a grandfather. No, it did not begin today or yesterday or the day before yesterday or even last week.

As a child the grandfather had learned that the earth is our mother. Before touching her, you have to breathe her breath, drench yourself in her energy, and ask for her permission with reverence, respect and ceremony. You can't pierce our Mother Earth's skin without first asking for permission and offering a few gifts from the heart in exchange.

Naturally, there's a huge party with candles, drums, marimba music and dancing to honor our Mother Earth on the day we ask her if it's all right to plant! First the Chuchu'ib' and Tata'ib', elders of royal birth, pray humbly and with simplicity, asking peacefully and calmly for permission to eat her fruits and live well. It's a solemn ceremony. The ageless male elders wear their most elegant outfits, blazing with ancient colors, and the women carry baskets of food for eating later. The smoke from the incense merges with the mist or makes the fog denser, and the dark colors of the elders' outfits blend with the brilliant plant colors, the sky and the reddening clouds. It's quite joyous, because when the festivities begin, the children run out to play, pretending to be teased, laughing right out loud, even crying because they are laughing so hard.

So you see that the cornfield that the grandfather was going to visit this morning, with Ixkem's hand clasped tightly in his, had a very ancient history. Its story merged with the mountain mist and glided down the stream of rivers whenever the sky filled with clouds — what we call winter clouds. At night these white tulle clouds work their way through woolen caps and make people cold and sleepy, then settle down on the hills.

The B'e'n *Appear*

THE CORNFIELD stretched out like a green lake for miles and miles. Because the grandfather could no longer tend it, he had brought together his daughters, sons and grandchildren a few days earlier. There were so many people in his hut that it was about to burst.

"Dear sons and daughters, I'm now one hundred years old. My hands and arms are tired, and so are my legs. For many years I've planted and harvested the fields on my own, but now the time has come for me to choose someone to take my place."

"It's a huge responsibility!" they all mumbled at once. Their hearts filled with sadness and their eyes with tears. They nervously awaited the grandfather's decision. Only he could say what the future would bring.

After a few days of discussion, pleading and prayers, the grandfather selected Ixkem, his youngest granddaughter, to replace him in the fields.

"But I'm too little!" she protested. "I'm really much too young."

"Neither age nor size has anything to do with it," the grandfather replied. "What counts is having the desire to learn from those who know more than you. We are all 'small' in knowledge; our desire to learn should be 'big'."

And that's how Ixkem was chosen to replace her grandfather as the caretaker of the cornfields.

And that's why on this morning they rose at daybreak and took the little path through the forest to reach the green cornfield. At one end there was a low mound where the grandfather stood to survey the crop, the gift of Ajaw, the Creator and Maker of our grandfathers and grandmothers. This was the best place to scare off parakeets, blackbirds, wild boar, squirrels, turtle doves, the smallest of worms and moths and even a few invisible insects who wanted to eat the corn. Now it would be Ixkem's job.

But how do you frighten off parakeets, blackbirds, wild boar, squirrels, turtle doves, the smallest of worms and moths and invisible insects? She only knew how to scare dogs away.

After her grandfather went home Ixkem looked around. She climbed the mound. "Well," she said, "I'll have to scare off the other creatures the same way I frighten dogs." And she started screaming, "GRRRRR! GRRRR! GRRRRR!"

From the edge of the forest, several sets of eyes curiously watched Ixkem's jumping and yelling. They belonged to the parakeets, blackbirds, wild boar, squirrels, turtle doves, the smallest of worms and moths and even a few invisible insects who were amazed that a screaming and yelling little girl had replaced the grandfather. They weren't frightened so much as intrigued.

"What if she hits us the way she screams?" they asked themselves. "Well, we better get out of here."

Ixkem's yelling and thumping was so loud, it reached the underworld.

Many *nahuales*, or spirits, live at the center of the earth, including some very special ones known as "*b'en*" in the K'iche' language. They look exactly like humans but are not human because they are *nahuales*. And they are very small — the size of a mango, an orange, an apple or a pear. The littlest ones are the size of tangerines, while the really big ones are as big as bananas.

Well, the *b'e'n* were working busily deep underground. They are very hard workers, which is why every once in a while the earth shakes.

So the *b'e'n* heard Ixkem shouting "GRRRRR! GRRRR! GRRRRR!" all the way up on the surface and decided to hold a meeting. The elders recommended calm and caution, but the youngsters insisted that more urgent steps were needed. Everyone who spoke had an opinion and seemed to have the right answer. But there were so many answers contradicting one another — one said this, the other that — that soon enough, the *b'e'n* were pelting each other with tomatoes. As always happens, the assembly decided to choose a committee to investigate the origin of the noises, messages, uproar and chaos up above.

Meanwhile, Ixkem was keeping an eye on things, "watching over the harvest," so to speak. She happily noticed how the green stalks changed color depending on the wind, the time of day and where the sun was on his journey across the sky. Sometimes the cornfield was a jade or emerald sea. At other times it wasn't a sea but an algae-filled lake.

The many sets of eyes watching the girl from the forest admired her, because she was the youngest grandchild. Even during lunch, Ixkem didn't stray from her lookout. She ate her tortilla with avocado and drank her buckbean juice without feeling a bit drowsy. There she sat, staring out over the huge field.

Soon some very small people resembling little men and little women, but who weren't little men or little women, started coming out of a little hole in the earth that Ixkem hadn't noticed.

It was the *b'e'n* committee.

The B'e'n *Meet with Ixkem*

A T FIRST Ixkem didn't see them. But then her eyes caught a tiny shadow sliding along the slimy mud. Something was moving down there!

She couldn't believe her eyes. Little people were coming out of the earth. They were the size of a pine cone, an average-sized pear or just about the size of a *zapote*. Elegantly dressed, the men wore hats, white shirts and black coats, and the women wore colorful *huipils* and dark wrap-around skirts.

"Who are you?

"What are you doing here?

"What do you want?

"Who sent you?

"Why are you so tiny?

"How old are you?

"Where do you live?

"What do you eat?"

Ixkem asked these questions as if she were a machine gun or firecrackers going off on a saint's day.

But the tiny *nahuales* kept calm. "Easy, little girl," they said, sitting in a half circle around her. "There's an answer to everything. And if we don't have the right answer, well, better not to ask!"

"My grandfather says that questions are important, but answers even more so," said Ixkem. She also sat down to be closer to the tiny *nahuales*.

It was a gorgeous day like many in the dry season in the Guatemalan mountains. Fat white clouds floated across the sky, and the sun hung above the volcanoes, giving apple cheeks to the children. The sky was blue and deep, and a calm silence hovered over everything. The soft cold gusts of wind barely stirred the tips of the pine trees growing on the sides of the dark mountains.

The *b'e'n* elders wore hats to protect them from the sun's rays, which are closer to the earth high up in the mountains. A kind of peace entered Ixkem's chest. The pure air had a nice aroma, like herbs or distant smoke or water bubbling up from a secret source or tamales wrapped in tender cornstalks.

"We also have lots of questions for you," one of the *b'e'n* said to her respectfully. "We've never heard such an uproar," he said. "And it seems that you, girl, whose name we don't even know, are the one responsible."

"Ixkem at your service."

"We are *b'e'n*," the man said, and he explained that they were *nahuales* who lived deep inside the earth. "We're ready to answer your questions, if you answer ours."

"What's bothering you, if I might ask?" Ixkem said.

"Everything!" the *b'e'n* answered all together.

Ixkem laughed. "Good! Now I know my grandmother was right. She was always talking about the world below. So we've got lots to talk about."

As they talked the sun slowly crossed the sky. The shadows were no longer just round balls under everyone's feet but now began to stretch and lengthen. By afternoon they would be gigantic.

The *nahual* who had spoken first stepped forward and took off his hat. "Well, I have a simple solution to what might be a thorny problem."

"Tell me," Ixkem said.

"You should come with us and tell us about life above the ground. We can feed you the sweetest fruit from the juiciest trees and give you lots of parties."

"I want to learn from you, too," Ixkem said, "in exchange for all I'm going to tell you."

The *b'e'n* made a circle to consider Ixkem's offer.

The young girl had forgotten that she was supposed to watch over the cornfields and that her grandfather would be very angry if she stopped her vigil. But she was excited to visit the underworld. She so much wanted to see her new friends in their own place.

When the *nahuales* had finished conferring, they said, "We accept your offer. You come with us and tell us about life on earth, and not only will we give you the most delicious fruits, the most fragrant flowers and the sweetest honey, but we will show you our life underground."

"But how can I go with you when your hole is so small?" Ixkem asked.

"All you have to do is stand in front of it," one of them said to her.

Ixkem bent down and tried to stick her head into the little hole. Just then the *b'e'n* gave her a push. Ixkem was scared as she felt her body sliding and tumbling down what felt like a tunnel of leaves. She bounced from side to side on the way down, but she was not hurt. This was a magic hole!

As she tumbled, she grew drowsy, yawned and finally fell asleep. She was still sleeping when she reached the kingdom of the *b'e'n*, the *nahuales* who live in the world beneath our feet.

19

Humans Are the Most Powerful Animals

WHEN IXKEM awoke, she was surrounded by the sweet-est fruit — Rabinal oranges, melons from eastern Guatemala, Antigua loquats, mangoes from the coast and Laj Chimel blackberries — the best fruit on earth. Not only was she surrounded by fruit, but also by the *b'e'n* Council of Elders who wanted to hear stories from above the ground, according to the agreement.

Ixkem knew so, so many stories that she didn't know where to begin. She sat down on a little seat of soft cushions made just for her so she'd be comfortable and calm as she spoke. Storytellers are always treated royally by the *b'e'n*, who are civi-lized and well educated, even though they are tiny.

"Okay," said Ixkem. "I'll begin with the story of how the lion found out that humans are the most powerful animals."

The *nahuales* sat down to listen.

THERE ONCE was a lion that walked through the jungle proud-ly and arrogantly because someone had told him he was the king of the animals. If a toad hopped by, the lion would kick him, and if the toad questioned him, the lion would answer, "I am the king of the animals and I can do whatever I want!"

The *b'en* opened their mouths like children as Ixkem began telling her story.

And that's how the lion lived, hunting gazelles when he was hungry and mistreating every creature that crossed his path. Each day his arrogance increased, until he insisted that every-one address him as "Your Royal Highness Lord Master Lion." Then he demanded to be addressed simply as "Your Excellency." And then he preferred "Your Most Serene and Royal Excellency."

He became so unbearable that the other animals called a meeting to complain about how the lion was treating them. A tiger told them all that the lion had bitten his leg just to show that he was the most powerful animal in the world. The turtle said that the lion had smashed his shell because he couldn't figure out where his head was. The mouse confessed that the proud lion had almost clawed him to death.

Everyone complained. Finally, the rabbit stood up and said, "My friends, I know how we can make the lion more humble."

The animals were happy to hear these words from the rab-bit, who was considered clever by them all.

"What do you think we should do?" they asked.

"My friends, there are creatures much stronger and more powerful than the lion. Humans — men and women — are much wiser."

They all slapped the sides of their heads. It was true! Men and women! Why hadn't it occurred to them before? Humans were more powerful than lions!

Just then the mouse, the elder of the group, stood up and said, "What the rabbit says makes sense, but who's going to tell the lion? A mouse? The proud lion would get so angry, he'd swallow him up in one gulp."

"Don't worry, I'll tell him," the rabbit said. He was as fearless as he was clever.

The other creatures were ashamed that the rabbit was the only one among them brave enough to tell the lion the truth. They all went back to their houses or their jobs and left him alone.

The rabbit went off to see the lion. "Good day, Your Most Serene and Royal Excellency!" the rabbit said cheerily.

The lion ignored him and went on cleaning and filing his huge claws.

"Ahem," the rabbit cleared his throat. "I said good day, Mr. Lion."

The lion looked contemptuously in the direction of the rabbit, who began to tremble. "Lowly rabbit, who are you? Where do you get the nerve to disturb me while I'm dedicated to the important task of filing my claws?"

"I'm a lowly rabbit!" the rabbit answered.

The lion seemed pleased. "I'm glad you recognize my greatness and your lowliness."

Silence followed. The rabbit didn't know how to start the conversation.

"What favor would you like? What praise do you come to offer? What gifts have you brought before me?" said the lion.

"Well, I come with nothing, Mr. Lion. I'm here to tell you about an ugly rumor that seems to be going around."

"Ugly rumor?" the lion roared. "Obviously about me! Those jealous, lying blubber lips!"

"That's how it is, Mr. Lion," the rabbit answered.

"Well, if you don't spit out the rumor, I'll wipe you off the face of the earth in a single stroke!"

"Yes, that's why I've come to see you," said the rabbit, shaking.

"Well, out with it!" the lion ordered.

"The word is that Your Highness isn't the most powerful creature on earth."

Before the rabbit could go on, an angry roar came out of the lion's mouth, and the whole jungle shook as if blown by a huge gust of wind.

The rabbit nervously hid behind a tree, wondering why he had put himself in this awful mess.

"Come out of there!" the lion shouted.

The rabbit reappeared, still shaking.

"I want you to tell me right now which creature is more powerful than I am."

"Well, word has it that humans are, Mr. Lion."

The lion laughed so hard that three monkeys fell out of the nearby trees.

"Now you'll see who's more powerful. I'm going to find a man or woman and I'll grab and eat him or her all at once," the lion yelled. And off he went to find a human.

It didn't take long. He soon found a woodcutter chopping firewood with an ax at the edge of the forest. The woodcutter aimed well and split trunks perfectly in two, four, six or eight pieces in a single stroke. The lion looked him over and decided that this little man with only two feet was nothing. He had no claws and needed a tool to cut wood.

"So you are a man," the lion said to him.

The woodcutter turned around. And then because he was very brave, he went on with his work as if nothing had happened. "Yes, I'm a man," he answered. "And what are you?"

The lion let out a roar that made the ax vibrate in the woodcutter's hands. Another couple of monkeys fell out of the trees.

As I said, the woodcutter was brave. Still, the loud roar unsettled him. To hide his fear, he asked, "My! What's making your throat so hoarse? Do you want to gargle with honey water?"

This comment further angered the lion who considered himself the emperor of all creatures. "I'm here to challenge you to a duel to see which of us is more powerful."

"Okay, if that's what you want," the woodcutter answered. "You'll just have to wait a little minute till I finish what I'm doing."

"Go ahead and take as much time as you need, as long as we fight so I can prove that I'm the king of the world."

The woodcutter wondered how he was going to get out of this jam. Then he had an idea. He looked at a half-split trunk, with his ax stuck in the middle. He made believe he didn't have the strength to finish splitting it.

"Mr. Lion," he said. "Could you give me a hand? If you help me, then I can fight you."

"I'd be happy to," roared the lion. "How can I help?"

"Why don't you put your paws right here in the middle. With the strength of my ax and your powerful muscles, we'll easily be able to split the trunk in half."

"Why of course!" the lion said, putting both paws in the split. Just then the woodcutter pulled up the ax and the trunk snapped together on the lion's paws.

"Ow, ow, ow," the lion cried. "I'm trapped. I can't get my paws out."

The woodcutter was dying of laughter. "What a stupid lion. You fell into my trap like a blackbird!"

"Oh, oh oh," the lion wept. "Mr. Woodcutter, please set me free."

"No," he answered. "You're a proud and vain creature and deserve to be punished. You wanted to know who the most powerful creature in the world was and now you know. And perhaps you've also learned a lesson in humility."

The woodcutter went off into the forest singing a tune to himself.

As the lion sat trapped in the tree trunk for days, the other creatures came by to see the spectacle of he who had been their emperor, tyrant, king and royal highness. Naturally, they made fun of him. The monkeys flailed him with their tails, and the elephants squirted water at him through their trunks. The turtles tickled him so hard that instead of laughing, the poor lion burst into tears.

Finally, a woman walked by. When she saw the lion's predicament, she felt sorry for him.

"Lion, why are you stuck like that?" she asked him.

"Because I'm vain and believed I was king of the world. I came to challenge the woodcutter to a fight and he defeated me with his intelligence. Now I'm trapped in this trunk, dying of thirst and hunger. Ma'am, won't you please set me free?"

The woman picked up a stick from the ground and stuck it in the crack. She pried the trunk apart and set the lion free. He couldn't believe it; a woman had used her brain to free him.

"Thank you, Ma'am," the lion said. "I now know that men and women are the most powerful creatures on earth. How can I repay the favor?"

"The only thing you can do is to be more humble and recognize that we all have our limits. Pride isn't just assuming you're better than the rest, but in thinking only about yourself. Without the help of others, we're nothing. If I hadn't helped you, you would've remained stuck there for the rest of your life. Let this be a lesson to you."

And so the lion went back into the jungle, kind and humbled. And he proclaimed to whoever would hear him that men and women are truly the wisest and most intelligent creatures in the world.

People Are Very Small When They're Born

THE *B'E'N* WERE so pleased and happy with the story of the proud, arrogant lion who learned an important lesson that some of them clapped.

Ixkem shifted in her seat. "You do know that men and women aren't always so wise and powerful. Before coming into the world, a baby spends nine months in his mother's belly, happy and protected, without worries or surprises. He swims about, surrounded by a sea of sweetness and dreams. Noises from the outside barely reach him. And when he comes out of the belly, we say he's born. The cold air enters his lungs, hurting him a little. He lets out a huge howl, as if he knows that the life awaiting him won't always be happy, and that he'll have to face great challenges many times."

The *b'e'n* had never experienced such things as birth themselves since they were spirits of nature. They were amazed to hear that humans were born crying!

"In the Maya village of Chimel," Ixkem went on, "babies come into this world assisted by a very wise woman who helps

the mother and the child. She is called an Ajkun, or midwife. My mother is an Ajkun who brings many boys and girls into the world. She has very long fingers and huge hands. Her job is a very pleasant one because it consists of filling the world with children, or in other words, filling it with life.

"When a child is born, the Ajq'ij is called. He is a guide who helps humans with the fate that will accompany them their whole lives.

"The Ajq'ij comes and invokes our Creators and Makers by burning *pom* incense. He then takes a few *tz'ite'* seeds, which are like little red beans, from a tiny bag. *Tz'ite'* seeds are sacred and are used to see the future.

"Then the Ajq'ij tosses the *tz'ite'* seeds onto the ground and, depending on how they fall, he is able to interpret the child's future. He also knows at once from the *t'zite'* seeds what the child's *nahual* will be."

"And what is a *nahual*?" one of the younger *b'e'n* asked. The others laughed because they themselves were *nahuales*.

"My dear *b'e'n*, I hope I don't confuse you by my explanation," said Ixkem. "A person's *nahual* is a little creature who represents that person in the natural world. Each time a person is born, his *nahual* is also born."

"Each and every single time?" asked a particularly mischievous *b'e'n*.

"Yes, of course," Ixkem confirmed. "Each time a boy or girl is born, a little creature is born who is just like the little boy or girl."

"And can the *nahual* of a boy or a girl be a rabbit?" another *b'e'n* asked.

"Yes," Ixkem answered. "It can be a rabbit."

"And can the *nahual* be a kitten?" still another asked.

"Sure," Ixkem said. "It can be a kitten."

"What about an elephant?"

"Or an ant?"

"A baby pig?"

"A porcupine?"

"A puma?"

"A little mouse?"

"A cockroach?"

They all laughed at that.

"And can it be an anteater?"

"A *pizote?*"

"What about a *taltuza?*"

"Can it be a…?"

They named animals as if they were standing right before their eyes. Ixkem was truly surprised that the *b'en* knew so many of nature's creatures, and that they knew them by their rightful names and could pronounce them correctly. The list went on and on till they had mentioned every single animal.

"A *nahual* can be any animal at all," Ixkem finally said.

Then one of the *b'en* exclaimed, "So if a child has a baby pig for a *nahual*, then he's going to become a baby pig?"

Once again they all burst out laughing.

"No, no, that's not how it works," Ixkem said. "For the Maya, each animal has a mission — qualities and purposes — that only our spiritual guides know. This is a big secret. If someone has a rabbit for a *nahual*, he won't necessarily be the fastest runner. Or if a turtle is someone's *nahual*, he won't be the slowest. The purpose of *nahuales* is reflected in humans who also have a special, secret mission.

"The *nahual* of each person is a secret. Only our holy elders, men and women who are our spiritual guides, know them. They tell the parents who keep it secret until the boy or girl is old enough to understand and guard this secret. And once they know they don't tell anyone, so as not to injure the creature representing them. This is why the Maya respect all animals, because each one represents a human being.

"And once they know what the *nahual* will be, the spiritual guides and the parents take the baby's umbilical cord outside. If they want the boy or girl to stay in the village, they bury the cord near the house. This will ensure that the person will stay at home. If they want him to travel by air, they hang the cord from the highest tree branch. If they want him to travel by water, then they throw the cord into the river. And if they want him to be a guide, they hide the cord in a secret place.

"These secrets are guarded like treasures because our lives are inside them," said Ixkem.

The *b'en* were very happy to hear these revelations. It was to hear these things that they had convinced Ixkem to visit their underground kingdom.

There Are Good and Bad People

"I f people are the smartest and most powerful creatures in the world, does that mean they are also the best and most virtuous?" asked one of the *b'en*.

"Not necessarily," Ixkem answered. "We Maya believe that everything has its counterpart. There's water because there's fire; there's sky because there's earth; there's man because there's woman. The large exists because of the small and the good exists because of the bad. Everything has its opposite. So there are good people as well as bad."

"And what do bad people do?" another *b'en* asked.

"Many things can make them bad, but craving, wanting what others have, is the worst — stealing someone's money, for example, or speaking badly of someone, which is the same as stealing his honor. If people weren't interested in having more, there'd be less evil in the world," Ixkem said.

There once was a young man who wanted to be an Ajq'ij, a spiritual guide. He approached the village elder and asked him to teach him the secrets of the plants, the secret of telling the future with *tz'ite'* seeds, all the secrets on earth. Since he was courteous, the elder decided to accept him as a student.

They began to study the forest plants: *chipilín*, wormseed, *pericón*, star palm, basil and even parsley. As they studied, a messenger came up to the young man and said, "Return to your village. A relative is looking for you and wants to give you a beautiful outfit!"

The young man hurried home and, sure enough, a relative was visiting who gave him one of the most beautiful Indian outfits in the region.

When he returned, the elder said to him, "My son, I see that you've been given a beautiful outfit. Actually, I need a colorful skirt to complete my outfit. Will you give me yours?"

The young man answered, "Sorry, teacher, but if I give you my skirt, my outfit will be ugly. Maybe sometime in the future I'll be able to give you a skirt."

So the two of them returned to their study of plants. The elderly spiritual guide also revealed the secrets of the mysterious fountains that spring forth from deep in the mountains; the meaning of the *pek* and of altars; why river stones glow like new when the sun shines through the foliage; the reason that rivers flow downstream to the ocean from the highest peaks.

This is what they were doing when another messenger arrived and said to the young man, "Return to your village because some wizards have come from afar and are giving away precious jewels!"

The young man ran to his village and, sure enough, he met one of the wizards who was speaking a strange, complicated language and was giving away pearls, topazes, rubies and emeralds. The young man received a bagful of precious jewels.

When he returned, the elderly guide said to him, "What

luck! My necklace just broke and I've lost a piece of jade. Would you give me a topaz, a ruby, an emerald or any old piece of jade, our ancestral stone?"

"Oh, master," the young man answered him. "I've already decided to give these jewels to my family. The topaz is for my aunt, the ruby for my mother, the pearls for my sisters, the emerald for my father, and I want to save the coral for a future girlfriend."

The young man had nothing to give his elderly teacher.

So they continued with their studies. The teacher told the young man the mysteries of animals, the value of birds and all the lessons to be learned from the forest and jungle dwellers — for all animals are wise and can teach humans many things. This is what they were doing when yet another messenger showed up.

"Return to your village because a government emissary has come and wants to make you the judge, not only of the province, but of the whole region."

The young man hurried home and was met by a government delegate from the far-off capital who was carrying some special scrolls. The delegate told him that the country's Council of Elders had decided to name him Chief Judge of the Province.

The young man put on his new outfit and a necklace with all the valuable jewels and took up residence in the Hall of Justice. He began to give orders and establish new laws. Then he remembered that there was a man in the region who was even wiser than he. This was the elderly guide, the Ajq'ij, his teacher.

"But surely there is no one wiser than me," he exclaimed. "By now that old man has taught me everything he knows and there's nothing more to learn."

So he ordered that the Ajq'ij be arrested. The police brought the old teacher before the judge, his former student.

"We're sending you to prison for practicing witchcraft!" he told the elder, without looking him in the eyes. The young man was arrogant, ungrateful and mean.

Grief-stricken, the old teacher stared at him. "You are unworthy of my teachings," he told him.

He gestured with his hand and the Hall of Justice, the village, the jewels, even the fancy outfit that the young man was wearing disappeared. All of a sudden the teacher and the evil student, who was now naked, shrunken and ashamed, were alone in the forest.

"I gave you all my wisdom and you weren't even able to give me a skirt for my outfit. I taught you the forest secrets and you weren't able to give me a single jewel. As soon as you had any power, you sent me to jail. You don't deserve my teachings," the elder repeated, "and that's why you will now forget them."

He gestured again, and the young man forgot everything the elder had taught him. His craving had made him evil.

"There are some bad people with lots of power," Ixkem said. "They declare war on others, they enslave their fellow man, and they don't know how to share their wealth. Of course there are good people who fight for peace, set slaves free and give to others. The future of the world depends on these good people," she concluded.

There's Magic in the World

"THERE'S MAGIC in the world," Ixkem said, "that makes women and men happy. This magic makes the world a more entertaining place and fills it with color."

THERE ONCE was a Maya couple who loved each other very much. They had been married a long time, but since they were from Chiquimula, they spent a good part of their days singing and enjoying the wonders of life. That's how people from Chiquimula are — the name itself means "goldfinch." And just as goldfinches hop from branch to branch, this couple would go from village to village, singing and eating what was given to them and sleeping wherever they were when evening came. Songs, flowers and love filled their lives. And they would say to one another, "We have come into this world only to sing. We have come into this world only to scatter flowers."

And that's how the years passed. And after so many flowers, so many songs and so much love, they decided they wanted a child.

"A child with our name," said he.

"A child who will be our namesake," said she.

"A child to bring happiness to our old age."

"A child to give us lots of grandchildren."

"A child to extend our lives."

"A child to store our memories."

So they visited the elders, Ajkun and Ajq'ij, and expressed their desire to have a child.

"Oh, my children," they were told. "We're afraid it's too late. You've let too many years go by and now you are old and cannot have children. Everything has its time and its moment. You've let yours go by, singing and dancing, sleeping under any old tree. You've crossed mountains and meadows and hung from trees as if you were monkeys, eating whatever was given to you, hopping from branch to branch like the goldfinches that you are."

They couldn't have even one child!

From one day to the next, the grief-stricken woman became old. Her hair turned white, her teeth fell out, and wrinkles of sadness spread all over her face. The man grew hunched and needed a cane to walk. Even his mustache turned white.

And they stopped singing, because life had suddenly become sorrowful.

Each day their house grew colder. Only the fragrance of flowers would encourage them to exchange a kiss or two every once in a long while.

And so the months passed. Then one day the man went into the forest to pick flowers for his wife, because he still really loved her as she loved him. He kept sighing and his sighs were complaints. He plucked a flower here, another there, until he had a bouquet. He was about to pluck a *quebracho* flower when suddenly a hummingbird appeared and began sipping the honey from the flower. The man stopped and admired the marvelous tiny bird.

When the hummingbird had finished, the man plucked the *quebracho* flower and went home. He was surprised to see that the hummingbird trailed after him. He tried to hide behind a tree trunk, but the hummingbird wasn't fooled. He hid behind a bush and the same thing happened. He ran off and the bird flitted after him.

He opened the door and gave the bouquet to his wife. "The strangest thing just happened to me," he told her. "A hummingbird followed me all the way home."

"Let's see if it's still here," his wife said.

When they opened the door, the hummingbird was gone. In its place stood a handsome little boy.

"Did you see a hummingbird?"

The boy laughed. "I was the hummingbird," he confessed, "but I've become a little boy. There was so much love in the nectar of the flowers that you picked that I've become the child you wanted all along."

And without asking for permission, he went inside the house as if it were his very own. He had barely crossed the threshold when he grew some more and became a young man.

"My name is Laj Pa'x," he told them.

The couple's hearts welled up with happiness. They were so happy that they began to grow younger. Their wrinkles disappeared, their hair turned black again, and teeth reappeared in their mouths.

Laj Pa'x was a good worker. In twenty hours he built a very pretty house for all of them. He started to watch over the fields, which grew big, full corncobs, and he made sure his parents were always happy. He also brought them luck — everything he or his parents did turned out right. According to our grandfathers, Laj Pa'x was full of fertility, fortune, abundant riches and knowledge.

Life went along pleasantly like this until one day his parents said to him, "You've brought us happiness. You've told so many mysterious stories that have filled our hearts with joy. You've been a ray of light in this house. Now we want you to give us grandchildren so we can give them our names and call them 'namesakes,' which is what we Maya call people who share our names. We want little boys and little girls to fill our house with squawking noises, to make a mess all over, running, jumping, shouting, destroying and crying sweetly…"

"Dearest parents," Laj Pa'x began, "I've come to bring you love and happiness. If you want grandsons and granddaughters, so it shall be. And they will also have your names."

That evening the mother fell into a deep sleep. She dreamt of her son, Laj Pa'x. In the dream he was carrying a large star that glowed in his hands. Laj Pa'x said to her, "Mother, this gift is the son you've waited for. I came because it was wrong for people who felt so much love to be so sad. Now you will have a child, who will be me, but in another form."

The following day, his mother was pregnant. His father and mother and Laj Pa'x were so happy that they began to travel, dance and sing once more. Laj Pa'x and his father took good care of his mother until the child was born — at the same time and on the same date that Laj Pa'x had come into their house.

The mother and father were so happy with the baby in their arms!

Then Laj Pa'x told them, "Mother, Father, the time has come for me to go. I've accomplished the mission our ancestors asked of me. Your love produced a son. I only came ahead to provide a kind of consolation. I leave you my luck, my wealth, my happiness and my heart. I will take nothing with me."

He had barely finished his words when he turned back into an especially beautiful hummingbird. He flew in circles around the house, swooping down on the people he had known and loved. Then he flew into the forest.

His parents let him go, knowing full well that he had fulfilled the mission entrusted to him by the ancestors. They renamed Laj Pa'x "Tz'unun," or bird son, and placed a honey jar in their courtyard. Every once in a while, Tz'unun would appear in the shape of a hummingbird and drink his parents' honey. And if he didn't drink honey, he would drink the nectar from a flower, for that has always been the fate of humming-birds.

This was the grandparents' magic. It brought happiness into the world.

How Men and Women Marry Each Other

THE *B'E'N WERE* intrigued by the idea that some people
lived in couples above ground.

"What does being married mean?" one asked.

"For what reason do they marry?" asked another.

Though Ixkem was just a young girl, she had learned a great
deal from her grandfather. At times it seemed as if he actually
spoke through her. This is why she could answer the questions
of the *b'e'n.*

"Well, men fall in love with women and vice versa," she
began to explain. "But not all women fall in love with men nor
men with women.

"Falling in love is a kind of miracle. It's magical when a man
feels love for a woman and a woman feels love for a man. No
one can explain why it happens.

"While girls are washing clothes in a lake or river, the boys
are watching. Between glances and laughter, love is born as
quickly as sunlight flashes on the water. If a boy likes a girl, he
goes up to her and flips her braid, just to fool around. She tells

him to stop and that's when they start to talk to one another."

"And what's love?" one of the *b'en* asked.

"It's when you see the best of yourself in another person," Ixkem answered. "Beauty, goodness and generosity."

"And what happens if a girl likes a boy and he likes her back?" another asked.

"In Chimel, my Maya village, the boy talks to his parents and tells them he's in love with a girl and wants to marry her. Then his parents go to the elders and ask them to speak to the girl's parents.

"On that day, a big party is thrown. First the grandmother and grandfather, who will be the guides, and the boy's parents, dressed in their finest clothes and carrying gifts, go one after the other — like army ants stealing garden flowers or announcing the rain — to ask for the girl's hand in marriage.

"The girl's parents welcome them and offer drinks and lots to eat. Then they party all day long. The young man's parents explain that he's in love with their daughter, and they humbly ask for her hand in marriage. And then something very special happens: her parents say no. That's how it has to be. The first time they ask for her hand, the parents must say no.

"The young man's parents hold huge ceremonies and observances, knowing ahead of time that this would happen. Then a year goes by when the lovers are boyfriend and girlfriend, but they still can't get married.

"At the end of the year, his parents ask to speak to her parents again. And once again, on the day of the request, the guides lead a procession of the young man's family, dressed in their finest clothes and carrying sumptuous gifts, to the bride's house. Her parents happily receive them, having prepared chicken soup, tortillas, party treats, candies, hibiscus ice tea, a bit of *cuxa* and other drinks. And once the introductions are over, and the young man's parents have asked for the young woman to become the wife of their son, what everyone was expecting happens again: once more her parents say no.

"That's how it is. The groom is rejected twice. His parents hold huge ceremonies and observances, knowing ahead of time that this would happen.

"And another year passes. During this period, the young couple has time to really get to know one another, to make sure that their love is real or to see if it is simply a flash in the pan, the flight of a wasp or the caress of a fly.

"But if the love isn't simply a flash in the pan, the flight of a wasp or the caress of a fly, then his parents ask to meet with her parents for a third time. And this time, the groom's parents head for the bride's house dressed up even fancier than before, bringing even more gifts. And they are received by her parents with more and better food: not chicken soup, but rooster in fermented corn soup or turkey in green sauce or large stuffed peppers and tamales, hot chocolate and alcoholic beverages and desserts, like glazed sweet potatoes, *chilacoyotes* and marzipan.

"And for the third time, they ask for the girl's hand in marriage. What everyone was expecting happens again: the parents of the girl say yes! Firecrackers are set off, the grandmother talks privately with the bride, the grandfather talks privately with the groom, and everyone dances on a carpet of pine needles. The parents, who are no longer parents but now in-laws, hug each other, and the bride and groom politely embrace one another. The happiness can be heard all the way to the edge of the village.

"Setting the wedding date is the only thing left to do.

"When the sweethearts marry, the wedding lasts all day. First the Ajq'ij escorts the couple to a large mountain altar. Then they go with relatives and godparents to the Catholic church where the priest celebrates Mass and the marriage sacrament.

"Afterwards, everyone goes to the bride's house and another ceremony as long as the Mass begins. The newlyweds kneel down on the ground and all the couples in the village walk past them, dropping flower petals on their heads and sprinkling them with advice from their own experience.

"The youngest couples with the least experience go first, followed by middle-aged couples, who know a bit more about what it means to be husband and wife, and last of all come the elders, who spend lots of time telling them that love is like the surface of a lake in the late afternoon. It changes color and tone and isn't always the same. At first it's the color of fire, turning the peaceful waters red. Then it turns orange, then rose-colored and gold, till it finally ends up white, lit up by the stars and the moon. It's always different and always beautiful.

"After the ceremony, in which the spiritual guides bless the couple, another huge party begins with more food, dancing and drinks. Everyone toasts the happiness of the young couple, because they know that a very long journey has begun and it's good to celebrate love. It is like a solid house added to the village, making it even happier.

"And the newlyweds begin to fly through life, building new nests."

The Story of the Man and the Thorn

"Not all people are happy," Ixkem explained to the *b'en*. "There are men and women who are so unhappy, sometimes they don't even know why."

One of the *b'en* nodded and said, "Happiness is a precious stone we carry in our hearts, though we might not know where it is."

Another elder said, "You can't seek happiness. You can only feel it. Those who seek it do so because they don't realize they already have it."

Still another elder added, "They go on and on searching, till they lose patience, convinced they've lost it."

"Happiness," said Ixkem, "isn't about doing cartwheels of joy, though that sometimes happens. Happiness comes from having peace in our hearts and from the love that others know how to give."

"That's true," said the *b'en* elders.

There was once a good man in Chimel who supported his family by selling oranges from Rabinal. Rabinal oranges are gorgeous — like tiny colorful suns hanging on trees. Best of all, they taste as sweet as a small drop of honey.

This man was returning from Rabinal with his cargo of oranges, but he didn't make it all the way back to his village. He stayed up on the mountain, in a cave. Each time someone approached, he would threaten them with a stick. This wasn't an idle threat, because several times he struck people who came into the cave where he was hiding.

Because of this, he developed a bad reputation in his village. In time, people stopped looking for him. He remained grumpily in his cave. Every once in a while his screams of pain and anger could be heard, and his family wept because they missed him.

Though the man seemed to hate everything in the world, some villagers thought he was just scared of people. The mayor decided to organize a delegation to try to convince him to come home. The delegation went along a very narrow path, wide enough for just one person, to meet him in his cave above the clouds and the pines. They chanted and burned *pom* along the way.

They started off happily and in a good mood, telling jokes and teasing one another as they went along. Soon, however, they tired of the climb and grew so quiet that the somber silence of the mountains overtook them.

They heard the wind whistling through the ravines, as it stirred flowers, plants and trees, and the occasional cry of a creature in the distance, from who knows where. They heard a bird singing, before its song faded behind a mountain, and the fresh gurgling of a river, evoking purity and clarity. There were also times when they heard nothing but their footsteps crumpling leaves as they walked. They felt the weight of clouds and sky, which gave them a kind of harmony. At these moments they sensed the utter majesty of the universe.

Finally, they reached the cave. When they saw the man, they could hardly recognize him. His hair had grown down to his waist and his beard fell over his belly. He wore lambskin because it was so cold up there.

As soon as he saw the delegation, he began screaming and throwing rocks. He chased after them, threatening to give them a good beating. The group scattered and returned to the village quite sad, saying there was no hope for the man — he had become evil.

But a little girl decided to look for him on her own. She followed the path of the adults up, up and up onto the mountain, until she too reached the evil man's cave.

He was asleep, tired from the fuss he had made earlier. She looked sadly at him, but she wasn't afraid. He looked so lonely and neglected. Under his lambskin, he still wore his old outfit, though it was now soiled and ripped. His feet were dirty and his toenails long and black.

As she gazed down at his feet, she understood what was bothering him. He had a big thorn sticking out of the bottom of his big toe. He couldn't see it.

This is why he is angry and in such a bad mood, thought the little girl.

Just then the man woke up and saw her. "What are you doing here, foolish girl!" he roared with all his might, so loud he could have frightened a tiger.

The girl knew what was wrong and wasn't afraid.

"I came to say hello. It's been ages since you've been to the village."

"I don't want to see or talk to anyone. I just want to be left in peace!" the man yelled.

The girl stood near him. With a quick move, she reached out her hand and *pop!* pulled out the thorn.

The man screamed so loudly that the sound echoed through the village, around the nearby mountains and went all the way to the bottom of the river.

"Owwwww! What have you done, you stupid girl!" he screamed. He then picked up his club to whack her.

"I pulled out the thorn that was causing you pain," she told him.

And just as the man was about to hit the girl, he began to feel relief. It was as if a fifty-pound bag of oranges had been taken off his back. He felt so much better that huge teardrops rolled from his eyes. He let the club fall to the ground, sat on a rock and sighed.

"Young lady, for the first time in months, I feel at peace. How can I repay you?"

"Come home to the village and your family and give them the love you've held back all this time," the young girl answered.

"But what's love?" the man asked. "I think I've forgotten its form, music and texture."

"Love is like the sweetest Rabinal orange, one that you carry in your heart!"

When the man came down from the mountain holding the young girl's hand, the villagers were astonished at the miracle she had accomplished. The man cut his hair and cleaned himself up. Then he gave each person a shiny orange full of the sweetness he had regained once the thorn that had caused him such pain was gone.

"You see," said Ixkem. "Sometimes only other people can see what is tormenting us and help to alleviate our suffering."

The Girl Who Lost the Light in Her Eyes

THAT AFTERNOON — which was really several afternoons
and nights later, because time cannot be measured in the
kingdom of the *b'en* — Ixkem told lots of stories. Some of them
will remain secret, because not everything has to be blasted over
loudspeakers to the four corners of the world.

One of the stories that the *b'en* liked most was about the girl
who lost the light in her eyes.

ONCE UPON a time there was a girl in Chimel who would go
to the river every day to wash her clothes. One day, as she was
getting ready to begin washing, she heard a gust of wind, or
perhaps it was the song of a bird or the rustle of leaves. It happened quickly, like the blink of an eye or a shadow crossing the
mind. It distracted her, as if she had fainted for a split second.
And when she regained consciousness, she saw her face reflected
in the river and realized that she had lost the light in her eyes.

Everything still looked the same. The green trees still bent
over the water; other trees higher up in the mountains were still

dark; the water was transparent; the rocks smooth; the underwater plants tiny. Everything was the same and yet totally different, because now there was the bitter taste of sadness.

The girl gazed into the water and saw nothing shining in her eyes. She looked again at the trees, plants, water and rocks. Everything seemed to have lost its glaze of happiness.

It was true. She'd lost the light in her eyes.

She dove into the river to look for the light. There she met tiny minnows that swim rapidly in mountain waters.

"Little fish," she began. "Have you by chance seen the light in my eyes? It fell somewhere around here."

"No," the fish answered. "We haven't seen any light."

And then she encountered a turtle swimming swiftly and deeply near the river bottom.

"Little turtle! Have you by chance seen the light in my eyes? I was about to wash my clothes when it fell into the water."

"No," the turtle answered, lazily lifting her old woman's green face. "No light has crossed my path."

The girl grew desperate. Then she saw an alligator yawning, showing the hundred thousand teeth in his snout.

"Mr. Alligator," the girl exclaimed. "Have you by chance seen the light in my eyes? I lost it somewhere around here."

"Oh, my sweetie. Do you expect me to go around looking for light when what I truly need is a good snack to eat in peace?"

The girl began to cry. Her tears couldn't be seen since she was in water. She asked the rocks, but they had seen nothing. She asked the river shrimp, the crabs, the snails, the tadpoles, the frogs and the toads. No one had seen a thing.

Where was the light in her eyes?

At the very bottom of the river she met the River Spirit.

"Come here, girl," the River Spirit called to her.

She swam quickly, making bubbles and stirring the water, hoping that the River Spirit had found the light.

"You found it! You found it!"

"Sorry, but I don't have it," the River Spirit replied. "However, I do have some advice. Go back to your village and ask your elders for the light in your eyes. Then ask your mother, your father, your brothers and sisters and your friends. Maybe this way you'll find what you've lost."

The girl climbed out of the water and walked back to her village. Somehow she found it a long and hard journey, ten times more difficult than she remembered. On the way she saw a world bathed in sadness. Colorful flowers looked ugly to her. And the little houses with smoke coming out of the chimneys seemed narrow and gray.

When she arrived home at last, she said, "Mamá, I lost the light in my eyes in the river. The River Spirit told me you would help me find it."

Her very wise mother lent her her own eyes. "Here, daughter of mine, take my eyes. Use them to see."

The girl put on her mother's eyes and a miracle happened. In the mirror she saw a very beautiful girl, charming and radiant. She recognized herself. A wave of warmth filled her heart — through her mother's eyes she saw the light in her own eyes.

Then she went to visit her father. "Papá, I've lost the light in my eyes. The River Spirit told me that you would help me find it."

Her very smart father lent her his own eyes. "Here, daughter of mine, take my eyes. You'll see yourself through them."

So the girl put on her father's eyes and looked into the mirror. There was a little girl with a halo of light above her head whose eyes sparkled brightly. She felt extremely hopeful, with a great desire for the future to be happy and sweet. Oh, how her heart filled up like a honeycomb when she saw herself through her father's eyes.

Then she visited her brothers and sisters and each lent her their eyes. Through them she saw lots of things: a girl her size with beautiful hair and dark skin; a smaller girl with a heart the size of a bird's; a bigger girl whose hands offered warmth and consolation.

And then her friends lent her their eyes and she saw smiles through them. She saw herself from behind, from above and running through fields. These views, some of which lasted barely a second, strengthened her legs, warmed her blood and cleared her mind.

Finally, her own light came back to her eyes, and the anguish she had felt turned into peace, happiness and contentment once more.

"You see," Ixkem said, "the light in our eyes is nothing more than the reflection of the eyes of people who love us."

"Yes, yes," said the *b'e'n*, very happily.

Ixkem Says Goodbye to the B'e'n
and Reunites with Her Family

"Well," said Ixkem. "I believe I've told you a lot about life above ground. I haven't told you every-thing because there are secrets you should never reveal. It's your turn to tell me stories about life underground, but they'll have to wait for another day. I must go back to protect the crops my grandfather has entrusted to me."

The *b'e'n* agreed that they had heard enough and now had a good idea what life was like in the world above. They had learned that people are the smartest creatures; that men and women are born from the love of their parents; that they are born tiny, each with a *nahual* and with a belly button; that there are good men who can become bad and sometimes even good again; and last of all, that only the light of others can warm the hearts of each and every one of us.

"The time has come for us to take you back up to your world," they told her.

Carrying torches, they led Ixkem through the winding paths of the underworld. In the Mayan language they are called *siguanes*. They are very deep and twist and turn like a maze. You could easily spend your whole life walking through the *siguanes* without ever finding the way out.

Then all of a sudden they saw sunlight slanting in from an opening in the ground. Ixkem hurried, afraid that she was late getting back to the mound where her grandfather had left her.

"We made it," the *b'en* said. "If you follow this path, you will reach your house. But before you go, we will tell you a secret you can share with your grandfather."

One of the *b'en* approached her and whispered a great secret in her ear. Ixkem stored it in her heart. Later, she would tell her grandfather, as the *b'en* had instructed.

The *b'en* crowded around to say goodbye to her. They cried tiny tears, for the friend they had made in those few days had stirred their hearts. Ixkem patted each of them on the head, because she couldn't hug them — they were like very tiny dolls. Amid cries and goodbyes they parted ways, with the *b'en* promising to repay her one day by telling her stories about the world below.

Ixkem followed their instructions, and as if by magic she ended up in the cornfield that her grandfather had entrusted to her. She climbed on the mound from which she could see the entire field and stayed there till her grandfather reappeared.

"Ixkem, you finally came back!" the old man said, hugging her. "You spent thirteen days and nights in the kingdom of the *b'en*."

Ixkem was very frightened because she hadn't realized that so much time had passed. To her, it had felt like an afternoon or even a day, but not thirteen days.

"I can't believe I was gone so long," she exclaimed.

"Thirteen days it was," her grandfather said. "When we came to look for you at the end of the first day, we couldn't find you. We were very nervous, wondering if we had lost our youngest grandchild, the one we had chosen to watch over the cornfield.

"I prayed to the *nahuales* for you to return at once. I went to the center of the cornfield and invoked Ajaw, our Creator and Maker, saying, 'Father Sun, Grandfather Sun, Master of All Light, Master of the Powerful Energy of All Creatures, *Nahual* of the Clear and Transparent Road, *Nahual* of Light: show me the way. Give me the light so I can go without regret, without sadness after one hundred years of living and eating here. *Nahual* of Darkness, the place of my brother and sister creatures of the night, the place of our ancestors, with the power of the long roads I've walked down before. *Nahual* of the Wind, *Nahual* of the Clear and Transparent Waters, *Nahual* of the White Clouds, Guardian of Our Breath. O *Nahual* where the wind hides out and gives me the strength of life and hope. O Heart of Heaven who allows me to exist in the space of creation. O Heart of Earth who created me and sustained me with abundant corn, with all the riches of your energy, hopes and well-being!'

"And I concluded by saying, 'Sacred Fire, give me a sign so that I may know where my granddaughter Ixkem is. What can I do so that she will return and complete her mission of watching and protecting the sacred corn?'

"The Sacred Fire set off a huge explosion. WHOOOSH! It was a message only I could understand. And that's how I knew you were in the land of the *b'en*, that you'd gone to visit the *nahuales* under the mountains.

"You had gone," the grandfather continued, "for the *b'en* to tell you a secret. I am now one hundred years old and cannot go to the kingdom of our ancestors until I have eaten my last cob of corn."

Then Ixkem whispered the *b'en's* secret in his ear.

One by one all the people from Ixkem's family showed up to celebrate her return, for she had accomplished the mission her grandfather had entrusted to her. They thought it was to watch over the cornfield. But the real purpose was to receive the secret of the *nahuales* so that her grandfather, once he had reached one hundred years of age, would know the secret and could rest from his life's labors.

The grandfathers and grandmothers, the mothers and fathers, the sons and daughters, the grandsons and grand-daughters were happy to have Ixkem back with them. Then they went into the village to celebrate the grandfather's one hundred years.

The women dressed like queens. They put on beautiful *huipils* embroidered with huge yellow, red and blue flowers. One woman had a sun on her *huipil* and another the four cardinal points — north, south, east and west. Each image on the *huipil* symbolizes a sacred object to the Maya. They had *tocoyales*, ribbons of different colors threaded in their hair to form a crown. They resembled true royalty.

Around their waists they wrapped cloth skirts, woven in sacred patterns, which they held up with colorful belts. And since it was a bit cold, they wore *perrajes*, or shawls. And some of them also carried elegant *tzutes* folded on their arms. A *tzute* is used to wrap food or gifts and is embroidered with many beautiful colored images.

The men also put on their best outfits. They wore straw hats with bands of multicolored patterns and cotton shirts with colorful ribbons attached to their sleeves. Brilliant rainbow-colored bands held up their pants, which themselves were multicolored and elegant. And sometimes they wore short pants over their long pants, just for decoration and distinction.

They threw a splendid party for the grandfather, who was about to go to sleep forever after reaching one hundred years of age and learning the secret of the *b'en*. A stew of potato and turkey cooked in large pots, while in others beans bubbled up like the Volcán de Fuego erupting, tempting guests to quickly make a taco with the tortillas the women had on the *comal* over an open fire. Large peppers, stuffed to bursting, somersaulted in the tomato sauce; *chipilín* tamalitos offered eaters a delicious and restful sleep. Cambray tamales beckoned with their sweetness and purple edges as if asking to be swallowed up.

Glasses filled to the brim with corn gruel were passed from hand to hand.

The grandfather strolled off to the end of the cornfield, carrying the roasted corn that Ixkem had prepared for him. "This is the food of the gods," he said as he slowly ate the kernels. The grandfather thoroughly enjoyed the corn.

"Now I can rest," he said. "I'm one hundred years old and know the secret of the *b'en*. My granddaughter also knows it and can take my place for the next hundred years. I can happily close my eyes. All I need is for the marimbas to fill me with music."

He lay down under a cornstalk, closed his eyes and fell into the deepest sleep. He rested peacefully, knowing his granddaughter Ixkem was going to follow the path he had begun, and that the Maya people would live forever in the forests, in the jungles, in the mountains and on the coasts of Guatemala.